Red Light, Green Light,

Mama and Me

A MELANIE KROUPA BOOK

For my mama, with love –CB

For all the children's librarians in the Cape
who work with love and dedication –ND

Thanks to EF and JE at the WPL —CB

Text copyright © 1995 by Cari Best

Illustrations copyright © 1995 by Niki Daly

Orchard Books
95 Madison Avenue
New York, NY 10016

Manufactured in the United States of America
Printed by Barton Press, Inc.   Bound by Horowitz/Rae
Book design by Chris Hammill Paul

10   9   8   7   6   5   4   3   2   1

The text of this book is set in 15 point Horley Old Style.   The illustrations are watercolor.

Library of Congress Cataloging-in-Publication Data

Best, Cari.
  Red light, green light, mama and me / by Cari Best: pictures by Niki Daly.
      p.   cm.
  "A Melanie Kroupa book"—Half title page.
  Summary: After taking the train downtown, Lizzie spends the day at the public library, help-
ing her mother who is a children's librarian.
  ISBN 0-531-09452-9. — ISBN 0-531-08752-2 (lib. bdg.)
  [1. Mothers and daughters—Fiction. 2. Libraries—Fiction. 3. Work—Fiction. 4. City and
town life—Fiction. 5. Afro-Americans—Fiction.] I. Daly, Niki, ill. II. Title.
PZ7.B46575Re   1995
[E]—dc20   94-33010

Red Light, Green Light, Mama and Me

by **Cari Best**

pictures by **Niki Daly**

Orchard Books
New York

"Red light, green light,
one, two, three,"
I sing as Mama and I
hurry across
the morning street.

Around the corner.
Past the mailbox.

Down the dusty steps.
I run like mad to keep up
with Mama's long legs.

Here comes the train!
Roaring out of the darkness
like a hungry lion.
Mama takes this train every day.
But today is my first time.
I'm going to work with Mama.

The city is mirror shiny right in my eyes.
And there is so much noise I have to cover my ears.
But a man and his dog still keep on sleeping.
They are missing the blue sky and all the pigeons.
And Mama and me walking tall and proud
in the window of a giant building.

"Here's where I get my
  blueberry muffin," she says.
"Two muffins today, Lenny.
  Lizzie's coming to work with me."
I like when Lenny says I look
  just like Mama.

I skip and jump instead of walk.
Mama holds my hand tight.

Finally she says, "This is it, Lizzie girl. The Downtown Public Library." My mama must be the most important person in the whole city.

Inside Mama's library there is a Reading Room.
It is so quiet that I can hear my shoes clicking across the floor. And there are millions of books.
High, low, and in the middle, too. No wonder Mama is so smart. "Do you read all day?" I ask.
"Not *all* day," she says. "You'll see."

Down the hall there are lots of mailboxes. Mama gets
more mail than the President. "Toby, you're here
bright and early," she says to someone who's already
working. "Granny's caught the flu, so Lizzie's a
working girl today."

"Hey, Lizzie!" says Toby. "How about we all meet for
lunch? I have enough peanut butter and bananas for
you, me, and all the pigeons in the city."

"Can I come, too?" asks a teeny weeny voice from behind a great big desk. It's Flo. I recognize her voice from talking to her on the telephone when I call Mama at work.

All of a sudden a man with a mustache and hair like
a French poodle comes *skating* in! Mama says it's
amazing Albert. "You must be Lizzie," he says.
Mama says Albert knows everything.
"See you at lunchtime," we tell Albert on our way
to the Children's Room.

I know Mama's desk as soon as I see
the bumpy crocodile I made for her
last year. I see puppets and puzzles
and music and crayons. And a lot of
the same books that Mama and
I read together at home.
If I had Mama's job, I'd look at books
all day, smell them, and take home
all the ones with new covers.

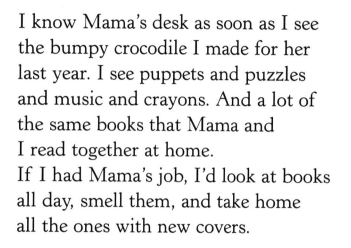

But Mama is way too busy to read to me now.
She talks and talks and talks on the telephone.
When she is finished, she comes running over.
"Lizzie, I'm going to tell 'The Three Little Pigs'
at story time. Would you be the Big Bad Wolf?"

I'm not sure if I can huff and puff like Mama does when she's the Big Bad Wolf at home. But I say okay anyway. I practice hard in front of the mirror.

Soon every pillow has someone
sitting on it. Mama looks beautiful
in her tiger lily dress and is
all ready to start, but I have
a thousand butterflies.
I listen for my part.

Then I HUFF and

PUFF and

BLOW the house down!

After the story Mama has a hug for everybody.
And a big one just for me. "I think it's about time
for the Big Bad Wolf to have lunch," she whispers.
"Working makes you *really* hungry," I say.

Out on the library steps, Toby, Flo, and Albert
are waiting to have a city picnic.
Toby's peanut butter lunch is good.
The pigeons love it!
For dessert I help Albert buy sky blue ices
from Luigi.

After lunch, while Mama does her reading work, Flo asks me to stamp a big pile of papers with today's date. Then she stamps my hand.
"Today is a very important day," she says.

In the middle of my stamping a little boy asks me which book he should choose. I show him where to find a really good one.
"This is the one *I* like best," I say.

Just then I see Albert waving to me.

"Lizzie, help!" he calls in a loud whisper.

Lizzie, Lizzie, Lizzie. *Everyone* needs me!

"This lady wants to know why pigeons don't fall off the
library roof when they sleep," says Albert.

Albert and I search a long time for the answer.
Finally we find it!

"'When a bird sleeps, its toes automatically lock around
wherever it's perched. And they don't open until the
bird wants them to.'"

"Like this," says Albert, closing and opening his hands.

I can't wait to tell Mama all about how pigeons sleep.
But first I have something very important to do.

I draw a little. Write a little. And cut out a lot.

When I am finished, I have a city of bookmarks:
one for Toby, one for Flo, one for Albert,
one for Mama. And one for me.

It's almost time for the Downtown Library to close.
I help Mama put back the puzzle pieces, the puppets,
and the chairs. Mama sticks her new bookmark
inside a big fat book on her desk. Right next to
the bumpy crocodile.

Downstairs, Toby, Flo, and Albert are getting ready to go home, too. When I give them their skyscraper bookmarks, they give me a giant work family *squeeze!*

Then Mama and I and all the other
work families in the city
say good-bye to the tall buildings,
the Lennys and the Luigis,
and the pigeons that sleep on the
library roof without falling off.

Red light, green light, Mama and me.